Troll of Tree Hill

An old-fashioned picture book for ages 8 to 108

by

Judy Large

Illustrated by Thomas Nelson

Hawthorn Press

Published by Hawthorn Press,
1 Lansdown Lane, Stroud, Gloucestershire
United Kingdom GL5 1BJ

Copyright © 1995 Hawthorn Press.

Typeset by Bookcraft, Lower Street, Stroud

Printed in Great Britain

British Library C.I.P. available on request

ISBN 1 869 890 74 4

ccording to old Scandinavian folk traditions, trolls were beings whose magic powers could be used only at night. On death, they were transformed into rocks and boulders which formed the landscape.

'In the old days, when only narrow, twisting paths wound their way through the moss-grown mountains of Norway, few human beings ever set foot there. The mountains belonged to the trolls, who were as old and moss-grown as the mountains themselves.

'There were many kinds of trolls: mountain trolls, forest trolls, water trolls . . .

'Biggest and strongest of all the trolls were those who lived inside the mountains. They had the strength of fifty men and they also had great magic powers and could throw spells over people. They hated the smell of human beings, the tinkle of church bells, and most of all they hated the sun. They were creatures of darkness . . .'

Ingri d'Aulaire
D'Aulaire's Trolls

I. Troll of Tree Hill

Great lashings of rain pelted down on Tree Hill that night, beating heavily on Troll's ancient rooftop until he snorted in his sleep and grumbled irritably at what sounded like beating on his door. The wind whipped up swarms of leaves and sent slender birch branches to and fro like fingers clawing at a dark, grey sky. The Stream at the Hollow Bottom rose steadily. Still Troll slept, snuggled in his warm sheepskin, deep down in the safe darkness of his gnarled tree trunk abode.

It had been his birthday that day, and in his dream hundreds of well wishers knocked repeatedly at his door and tiny window, wanting to be let in. 'Bah,' He told them. 'I've had my day already. Go away.' With a special snarl and a fierce grimace he snored loudly, hiding his head under his covers, dreaming now of the beautiful nut cake the animals had made for him. And on his nose was the new nose warmer the birds had woven for him, specially.

The end of Troll's nose tended to be cold. It had, he understood, very poor circulation (this being the result of an accident years – perhaps centuries – ago when he had caught it ungraciously in a slammed timber door when chancing too close to humans). He had pulled his nose free, of course, but it had never been quite the same since. He frequently rubbed it when thoughtful, not that it helped him think but it did warm it a bit. One wasn't quite sure whether Troll's reputation over the years as spread throughout the woodland (Troll knows (nose?) a lot) was due to repeated stories of his wisdom or his accident. But certainly he was respected.

Now lightning struck in the Hollow and in Troll's dream his cake dazzled with light as dozens of

beeswax tapers were lit on it – for no one knew Troll's age for certain. It shone like a star for him, and when thunder rumbled outside, for Troll it was the voice of his ancestors, the ancient ones, the grandfather and great-grandfather Trolls who had come and gone before him. 'Do what is right . . .' they mumbled, 'take courage and find your task' . . . mumble . . . rumble . . . through thick beards and a thicker haze of cloud-like mist the ancients sang to him of faraway lands and times of magic.

So Troll slept on, until the storm died away and only a steady drip from the trees could be heard. Pink and coral colours streaked the horizon, puddles glistened and the gurgling of the stream was morning music to the animals who crept forth now.

Kingfisher perched silently above the rushing water, watching intently for the silver glint which could mean fish breakfast. Little Doe tiptoed delicately through the mud, down the bank to drink. Dragonfly Blue darted from stone to twig – never quite deciding where to stay still. A family of moorhens swam dizzily further upstream amid swirling water, and Watervole peeked out of her burrow entrance below the roots of a dripping willow tree.

Watervole sniffed to smell the morning, decided it was good, and first scurried, then dived into the water. She emerged just below the narrow path that led to Troll's doorway. Ignoring the rising chatter of birds in the branches above, she tapped on the small, round window. 'Troll – time to get up, Troll. Troll, are you there? The rain's stopped, Troll.'

A clatter could be heard as someone indoors rolled over and knocked down the brass candle stick by his head. This was followed by a distinctive bellow. 'Who's there. Go Away!'

'Troll'. Watervole never gave up easily. 'Troll, you wanted to be called just after sunrise.' She peered through the dusty circle but could see nothing.

Inside, Troll stepped out of bed straight onto the candlestick. He slipped and went flying directly into his front door which burst open with a crash, making poor Watervole jump. 'Troll,' she said, peering intently at him as he lay face down in the mud, 'I didn't see you coming.'

'*GRYMNOSTGR*!' Came the muffled reply.

'Pardon?' asked Vole, who tried always to be a polite and caring creature.

Feeling confused, and not hearing well because of the bird chatter above, Vole decided to get help. Within moments a circle of animals surrounded the helpless, thrashing figure in the mud. They listened. Little Doe nodded. 'He says,' she pronounced solemnly, 'that his nose is stuck.' Startled to hear and now see this truth all the friends began at once to rescue Troll in a most earnest and chaotic fashion. Little Doe nudged his backside with her head. Rabbit and Watervole tugged at his jumper. Even Badger and Hedgehog plodded along to help. Troll emerged with a sudden popping noise and sat upright, rubbing his nose and sputtering. Soft damp leaves were offered him for cleansing, and Spider administered first class web to the small bump. When this help had been given, a silence fell on the group as they gazed, wide-eyed, at the rescued Troll.

'Well!' He demanded. 'What are you all staring at? And what is all that noise about?' He threw his head back to look upwards into the tree branches at the gathering throng of birds. 'You there! Stop fussing! I'm all right – no need to be so excited.' As Troll rose stiffly to his feet, down swooped half a dozen birds.

'It's Grey Wagtail,' they chirped. 'Grey Wagtail has gone missing. We think he was lost in the storm.' An anxious hush fell on the group.

Troll rubbed the end of his nose thoughtfully, twirling a bit of spider web around his finger. He was surrounded by worried faces. How often had they heard those dreaded words – 'gone missing' – in the wood. He thought of young badgers and foxes savaged by hounds, of rabbits and hedgehogs run over by ox carts on the road far below Tree Hill and this side of Down Yonder, of deer shot silently with bows and arrows. 'We must look for him at once,' he commanded.

Troll led the search for Grey Wagtail by walking round and round in the same small circle at the top of Tree Hill while animals and birds spread out into every possible corner and mossy verge. He stomped his feet steadily and clenched his hands behind his back. But he was not his strongest in daylight. He stopped often to sit hunched over on a rock near Kingfisher's fishing place. It was nearly midday when a patrol of moorhens reported a sighting; Grey Wagtail was on his way home, winging in on a cool breeze.

The animals were elated! Troll beamed kindly at Grey Wagtail as the yellow breasted bird came to rest at his feet. 'You have had a terrible time, my friend.'

'Troll –' began Grey Wagtail, but Troll's voice rose even louder:

'From out of the swirling depths of wind and rain – from the clutches of thunder in the Great Storm, you have returned to us.'

'Troll –'said the bird again.

'Don't try to tell us your story now,' commanded the older, bearded figure. 'We will gather at dusk and hear your story! A meeting at dusk at the stone circle!'

'But Troll –' Unheeded, Grey Wagtail hung his head. The woodland friends welcomed him home, and Troll trudged gratefully back to his resting place in the tree roots, where he slept all afternoon.

He awoke to supper of blackberries and hazelnuts, kindly provided by Watervole, and to the soft fading pink and golden light of an autumn afternoon. Leaves drifted slowly from branch to ground. There was peace on Tree Hill.

For as long as any of the animals could remember their relationship to the world outside had been ruled by Troll leaders. Tree Hill had its natural rules and laws of life and each creature learned these soon after birth. They knew that activity changed with the seasons, that the new born arrived in Spring alongside glistening new plant life, that killing in the animal Kingdom was acceptable only for obtaining

food, that the harshest trials came from human beings: metal traps, weapons, fire, or the deliberate destruction of woodland. Bears, wolves and beavers had disappeared since the coming of humans. They had died out in ancient times of Great Battles.

Trolls had been tall, strong and fierce then, capable of hurling thunderbolts out of a night sky, of opening up cracks in the hillside to prevent men crossing over. There had been many trolls, whole families of trolls, and they succeeded in keeping people off the hill, out of the remaining dense woodland. People had their kingdom Down Yonder. The animals had Tree Hill.

Now Troll was the only one of his kind remaining. Deer, rabbits, foxes and birds would take note (quietly) that he was not so very tall, perhaps not so very strong as those before him had been. They understood that he tried to be fierce and wise. Who else would look after and protect them when he was gone?

II. Revelations

Under a clear grey-blue sky lit by the first evening star and a slender new moon, the animals and birds made their way to the stone circle. Bats and Owl joined them now. Toads hopped through leaf mold and over fallen branches. Badgers romped playfully and even Old Otter appeared from a long distance away. He preened himself as Little Doe arrived, and gradually everyone found a place. They could hear Troll stamping his way through the trees with the gentle scurrying of Watervole behind him. Grey Wagtail stood patiently on a moss covered stone, and other birds perched eagerly on branches overhead. Rabbits, squirrels and mice assembled together in the evening shadows. Troll entered the circle importantly, and it was time for the meeting to begin.

They had last met at the stone circle for Troll's birthday, and came together frequently for celebrations or to settle disputes over acorns or fishing rights. Everyone loved gathering to hear about someone's adventure. Sitting now on his usual stone seat Troll raised his hand. 'Come Grey Wagtail. Tell us how you braved wind and rain, lightening and thunder. Tell us how you escaped the beating elements and –'

'Troll! Let him begin!' Suggested Little Doe, and all eyes fell on Grey Wagtail himself. The bird flew to sit on Little Doe's back so as to gain extra height, and then he began.

'I was not lost in the storm last night,' he said. A puzzled wave of murmuring rose among the crowd. 'I spent the night Down Yonder.'

There was a completely shocked silence. Troll sat, dumbfounded, not believing his ears. Blankly, slowly, he asked, 'What did you say?'

'I said I spent the night Down Yonder.'

Troll rose to his full (short) height and clenched his fists. His face was turning a deep reddish-purple colour. Everyone knew what was coming: 'YOU SPENT THE NIGHT DOWN YONDER!' Troll roared. 'HOW DARE YOU. *HOW DARE* YOU BETRAY TREE HILL AND ENTER ENEMY LAND? EVIL LAND OF HUMANS – EXPLAIN YOURSELF!' He bellowed with such force as to lift him six inches off the ground.

The circle of gathered friends cringed. Grey Wagtail began bravely. 'There is a lovely garden there where some children have made a bird feeder . . .'

'*Children*!' Screamed Troll, jumping up and down. '*Children do not exist*. HUMANS exist – evil, smelly, destructive vile enemy humans! There is no such thing as CHILDREN. Just big humans and little humans. They are all the same. Horrid creatures! They tempted Robin and Red Fox away to feed at their places of badness. Now you would join them!'

'Troll,' Grey Wagtail piped up, 'I just had to go. I had to see for myself what was on the other side of the road. It wasn't a place of badness. There were nuts and birdseed, and flowers, and a little stone bath with water in it.'

'*ENOUGH!*' Troll was enraged. All around the circle animals cowered, shook, waited. Then Hedgehog scurried forth.

'Troll,' came her tiny voice. 'I visited once too. I drank from a saucer of milk on a doorstep.'

Troll thought for an instant that he would faint, such was the shock of this. He rocked slightly on his feet, staring wide-eyed at Hedgehog's tiny form. An odd sputtering or choking sound came from his throat. Finally, he was able to steady himself enough to speak again. This was a deep, gruff speech with anger rippling through it.

'MY Ancestors followed humans from the Northern Place to these Lands, allowed themselves to be seen at times, wove their magic around the human spells and tried to live side by side. Humans rode horses, beat oxen, fought with each other, trampled fairy rings, *denied* gnomes and elves, ruined beautiful forest lands, hunted and killed every possible animal. We on Tree Hill will have nothing to do with humans, or their ox carts or vile battles. I have spoken.' He sat down, expecting complete respectful silence now. But another voice interrupted the quiet suspense. It was Little Doe.

'Dear Troll,' she began, 'you know I lost a fawn on the road at the bottom of Tree Hill last Spring.' (Everyone nodded solemnly, remembering.) 'We gathered here to mourn his death. Dear Troll, it was not an ox cart that ran him over. Oxen are alive on four legs, like I am! No human could beat an ox into trampling a fawn, surely, for we are a kingdom of animals! No, the blackbird who saw the accident said it was a square shaped hard box on four round forms which moved terribly fast and made a loud noise! It had a human inside it.' Little Doe's voice fell to a hush. 'Perhaps this monster had eaten the human,' she suggested, sounding frightened.

Troll's eyes narrowed and he sat tense as a brick. The evening's darkness had fallen and a grey cloud covered the silver moon. Nervous whispering and nudging rippled around the huddled group. Grey Wagtail and Hedgehog spoke together. 'It is true. There are no more ox carts. No more bows and arrows, no more rough fortresses with hounds on chains.'

That did it. 'ENOUGH,' roared Troll, leaping in crazed frenzy from his stone seat. '*I have heard enough.* Grey Wagtail and Hedgehog – you are both banished from Tree Hill as of tomorrow mid-morning. You will never set foot in these woods again.'

The two small figures in the center of the circle trembled. Rabbit ran to comfort them, and tiny groans and cries could be heard all around. Old Otter shook his head sadly, Little Doe wept and the sound of fleeing bat wings could be heard in the darkness. Watervole hid her face in her paws, unable to face it all.

Troll had finished. He turned his back on the cowering, sorrowing group. He walked around the stones and back to the pathway. The new moon reappeared just enough to partly light his way back to Gnarled Root House. He was wide awake with anger, and hurt, and memories.

Once back home, he lit the candle in his brass candle stick and remembered stealing it one such moonlit night from a hut near a castle wall. It was his trophy, his prize possession. The candles he made himself from wild beeswax. When Troll Woman had lived she had made them, and sewn his rough breeches and top, and baked hard sweet brown bread. A single tear pushed its way down Troll's long nose as he thought of Troll Woman. What would she have said about today's goings-on? There was a beautiful, round stone up the stream which reminded him of Troll Woman.

Troll felt very old and very stiff. Robin and Red Fox, Hedgehog and Grey Wagtail . . . who would be next? Why didn't they listen to him? He shook his head and stroked his beard, staring into the candle flame. In its flickering glow he saw again the tall flames of midsummer bonfires, heard the laughter of elves and gnomes float through the valley as clear as the chime of a crystal bell. Down yonder had been lush valley and marshlands. Deer and wild boar roamed freely, and wolves lived on Tree Hill then. At full moon the pastel forms of dancing fairies bade the wild flowers to grow. The men on horseback were welcomed at first. They had used their own magic to drain some of the marshes. They had created green meadows and put sheep in them. They planted corn which grew golden in late summer. (Troll men had often craftily gathered corn by night, and troll women baked small loaves deep in the wood.)

But other humans kept coming, fierce battles trampled the corn and ugly shouts and screams filled the air as huts and wooden fortresses blazed in angry fires. Troll put his face in his hands, remembering, remembering. He'd been carried as a tiny Troll – carried by his father out of a shimmering red haze of intense heat, past flying, swirling cinders and billowing smoke – carried to the safe haven of the

stream and Tree Hill. Only once again had he ventured Down Yonder, to fetch the candle stick by night as a wedding gift to Troll Woman. Children, bah! Humans big and little were the same; they thought they knew everything and could do anything. Small humans were just a trick and the animals were foolish simpletons if they thought otherwise!

The small glow of flame disappeared into a puddle of hot wax. Grunting and shuffling, Troll found his nose-warmer and put it on. He climbed wearily into bed, feeling his every joint creak. In a few moments he was snoring loudly, on his way to lovely, comforting dreams.

He awoke to knocking at the door – not Watervole's gentle tapping but a rather ferocious pounding' THUMP THUMP THUMP – 'TROLL!' came a shout. THUMP THUMP THUMP! Indignant, Troll sat up in bed. What was all this about, then?

'Yes, yes . . . what is all the fuss?' He muttered into his beard.

'Emergency, Troll! Troll- let me in!' It was Old Otter, looking slightly flushed. Whiskers shaking, he took a deep breath and began. 'Tree Hill has a visitor, Troll.'

Troll removed his nose-warmer carefully and slowly. 'What sort of visitor?'

'It's a small human, Sir. Grey Wagtail says it is a Child.'

The earth seemed to rush away from under Troll's feet. He clutched at the door and whispered, 'A small human?'

Otter nodded. 'It crossed the road from Down Under just after dawn. The bramble bushes and uneven rocks didn't stop it. It just kept walking and climbing.'

'Where is it now?' Croaked Troll, wishing he could be swallowed by a suddenly appearing hole in the ground.

'Down the stream sitting on a rock. We thought you should know so that you can see to it at once.'

'Yes,' gulped poor Troll, wondering why his stomach seemed to be wrestling with itself. 'Yes, I'll see to it.'

A sick, cold dread filled him as he dressed in his cloak and took his wooden dagger from its place on the wall. (Blowing the dust off it made him sneeze.) Sunlight peeked through his round window and dazzled him as he fumbled in his memory for the right magic. It didn't come. He didn't remember. He would have to directly confront the human, show it who was boss, frighten it off the hill. Yes, he would do that. He could do that.

Troll of Tree Hill strode evenly, head up, with bold steps when he left Gnarled Root House. He was well aware of the dozens of hidden eyes which watched him from behind leaves, branches, and fallen logs. There was utter silence in the wood apart from the steady padding of his feet. Old Otter stayed behind, waiting and wondering.

Down at the stream Watervole felt trapped and terrified even though she was well hidden in her mud home beneath the willow. There was no way she could run to warn Troll without directly crossing the path of the huge foreign creature which sat on the bank, splashing its feet in the chill-of-the-morning water. It had even eaten some blackberries. She had seen it! Kingfisher had flown well away, but Dragonfly Blue was hiding somewhere, watching with curiosity. On a branch above sat Puck the wood pigeon, bobbing his head from side to side in anticipation.

Troll's plan was simple. He would burst out of the bushes above the bank suddenly and silently. He would glare and raise his sword. The sheer sight of him would send the human running back to Down Yonder. He had seen this work before. It must work now.

The human looked up when an odd rustling could be heard behind the bushes. There was a sound like a muffled grunt. Then, slowly the branches parted and out stepped Troll. His cape was blowing in the wind, his sword raised, and there was a fierce glower on his face. Troll showed his teeth, pointed his slightly wobbling sword directly at the human and thought to himself, 'It's working . . . the visitor is terrified . . . it will turn and flee!'

'Why,' spoke the small human, 'is the end of your nose blue?'

Troll of Tree Hill blinked.

The little voice came again, 'Excuse me, but I was wondering why the end of your nose is such a very blue colour.'

Now Troll gulped, and stammered – 'The-the-the end of my nose is not blue! What are you doing in sacred hollow tree ground by *our* water!? You have no right to walk by this stream.' He drew himself up on tiptoes: 'You will leave at once or lightning will strike you on the spot! The stars will fall on your head and the thorn bush will scratch you!'

'The end of your nose is blue, you know.' To his utter horror Troll realised that the small human was moving in the wrong direction. It was walking towards him, not running away from him at all. Above them Puck the pigeon flapped his wings and flew off. Watervole peeked anxiously through her crack-in-the-earth bank window, nervously wringing her paws. The small human was not much bigger than Troll, and gazed solemnly as Troll brandished his sword wildly. 'Careful, you'll hurt yourself,' it said.

This took Troll so by surprise that he dropped the sword and collapsed in a confused heap onto a pile of leaves. He felt dizzy and was only slightly aware that the human was sitting down next to him. It spoke again. 'You do have a lovely beard, though, I wish I could grow one like that one day.'

Troll looked at him and blinked. 'You have started one already.'

'What?' It laughed, 'No, that's blackberry juice. I'm only a boy!'

A boy. Child was a boy, a small man. Troll sighed and rubbed his nose nervously. 'It gets cold sometimes, that's all. My nose, I mean.'

Pairs of hidden eyes watched the two small figures sitting in the leaves. Pairs of ears strained to hear what was said and to understand it, while far away down the hill, the unknowing Hedgehog and Wagtail began their perilous crossing of the dreaded road, on their way to exile.

III. Serenity Speaks

Child introduced himself and Troll did the same. 'Really?' asked Child, 'I thought trolls slept in the daytime and only came out at night. That's what the story books say. Are you sure you are a troll?'

'I am Troll of Tree Hill, Guardian of these Woods!' But inside Troll's memory something stirred . . . a faint, ringing glimmer of something. Had this been true of his ancestors? Was this why he tired so easily by day? Then flapping pigeon wings above reminded him of two things; that he was very important, and that he was defending the Wood from an invader. Troll rose and said very loudly, 'Come along, then. You are my prisoner, even though you want to run away.'

'Pardon?' Child asked, also rising.

'Follow Me!' bellowed Troll. The sound of his usual voice sent a ripple of relief through treetops and bushes as animals and birds realised that he was fully in charge, after all. Troll turned and took two powerful, mighty steps before he tripped over a tree trunk and rolled into a ravine, fussing and sputtering. When on his feet again, he shook dry leaves off in every direction, and continued forth. For some reason his feet took him back to his home but he wasn't certain why. As the morning sun climbed higher in the sky it danced and glinted through golden, orange and scarlet leaves on gently swaying branches. Some of the more playful leaves floated downwards to cover the roof of Gnarled Root House, while inside, Troll and Child ate hazelnuts with honey, drank wild mint tea and talked. Child answered very solemnly about ox carts – no, he did not have one, nor had he ever even seen one! But he had ridden briefly on a pony at the seaside. He had always wanted to come and explore these woods. It was searching for Grey Wagtail that had brought him today, but he would have to be home for lunch. He would keep the visit a secret – he really would!

When the sun was directly above the treetops Child said he must go. He put his hand into his pocket and pulled out a round glass ball covered in swirling yellow and blue colours. 'This is my best marble,' he said. 'Please have it as a present. And do please come and visit me sometime. Not many people believe in trolls anymore. I would look after you. You would be safe! Do come.'

Troll directed Puck to fly from treetop to treetop as far as the stream, so as to guide Child part of the way back. Then he said a gruff good-bye, clutching the marble in one hand. It was so round and smooth, this child-pebble. When he looked at it closely it seemed as though many colours played inside it in tiny waves. From down the path came the faint call 'Good-bye . . . come and see me . . . I won't forget you.' And then silence, only the treetops rustling.

Child hopped from stepping stone to fallen tree trunk, and to stone again to cross the stream. Then, hands in pockets, he gazed at his surroundings. Dazzling blue autumn sky, the giant willow and silver birch trees, soft leafy woodland floor, bramble bushes and rose hips. Not far away a kingfisher dipped into shimmering water for a fish. Child smiled. Then he whirled around and ran off towards Down Yonder.

As soon as he was gone Watervole emerged from her hiding spot. Two grey squirrels dashed down tree bark in playful scamper, and little Doe (whose soft brown colouring had kept her perfectly hidden in the shadows) stepped gently into a patch of sunlight. Dragonfly Blue flew from mud to tree root. Moorhens swam out from the rushes. Tree Hill felt normal again.

But the normal feeling was not to last. From the Hollow came curious crashing noises:

Thump! Wallop! Stomp!

Thump! Wallop! Stomp!

Someone was telling Everyone Else that he was in a foul mood. Quite wisely, Watervole stopped in her tracks, turned and disappeared back into her burrow again. This was obviously a day for safe hiding. Crash-Thump-Wallop-Stomp. Troll kicked a small tree stump and stubbed his toe, roared and then glared at the tree stump. He muttered and limped and stuttered. Troll was cross.

It didn't matter that it was a beautiful golden day, that juicy blackberries hung ripe and heavy on every bush. It didn't matter that he had a new shiny marble in his pocket. Troll's world had been disturbed, and he couldn't quite put it right again. His own private little thunder cloud seemed to follow him as he thrashed about restlessly all afternoon.

The animals and birds watched and listened calmly. Unless they were injured or sensed a sudden change in the weather, they did not, as a rule, have moods. They accepted Troll now as one would a brief storm. Most of them were busy preparing for winter, anyway – gathering in stores of nuts and grain or preparing soft, hidden sleeping places.

But the stomping noises continued the next day. Almost as though Troll had created them, real clouds appeared in the sky. Some were slate-grey and others cotton-wool-white. But Troll could not settle, could not quieten down, and on this morning he decided. He would journey to Upper Wood and seek out Serenity, the Wise One. He knelt on the bank of the stream and stared at his reflection in the ripples, noting that his beard was much longer and whiter than when he had last seen Serenity. His bald patch, bushy eyebrows and eyes, pointed ears and long blue-tipped nose all danced unsteadily back and forth in the moving water. Troll announced to no one in particular, or perhaps to his own watery image, that he was going.

Watervole appeared by his side almost immediately. She had fetched for him his woolly hat and offered it now. Troll nodded and put it on. He patted Watervole's head in thanks, and cleared his throat rather loudly. 'I'll be back when I am back,' he said gruffly. And then he was gone.

The way to Upper Wood was a winding path over large rocks and through dark dense forest. Troll trudged uphill, hardly looking where he was going. It was not even that he remembered the way. His feet simply took him. Occasional large single raindrops wetted his face, but he didn't notice them. He passed Old Otter's hiding place. He passed the entrance to Fork Cave, where long ago the gnomes had mined for beautiful, sparkling gems and crystals. He walked steadily, and with a lighter step as night fell, feeling that curious extra bounce that came with the evening. Each star that shone above him was a particular sparkle that he knew well. As the sky cleared, Troll's spirits rose.

All night long he walked until he was far away from the comfort of his own hill. Giant beech trees towered above him, their huge arm-like branches forming a forest ceiling. An owl hooted, several bats flew by, and there were rustlings here and there. On Troll walked. At dawn he sat on a moss-covered log to watch for the first morning glow in the sky. But as the sun rose a tiredness filled his bones again and the troubled, disrupted feeling returned. He knew every star in the sky, every bird and animal in his wood, every tree and each bend in the stream. But Child's appearance had changed everything, somehow.

This was what he explained to Serenity. She sat in her cloak of russets and yellows, with its dancing copper-red hues of autumn leaves. Her dress was a deep moss green, her hair the blue-black of starry night-time, glistening here and there where the morning light caught it through overhead branches. Her face was both as smooth as an apple and as wrinkled as a walnut, as brown as the earth and as light as the moon. Her eyes held as the deep colours of time, and she sat in the solid, throne-like roots of a giant beech tree.

Troll of Tree Hill had not been to her for years. He always felt better when he went, as though a warm mellowing happened inside his chest – a softening and a longing filled him, and then a gentle fullness. (It was rather like the feeling after a delicious hot drink on a bitterly cold winter evening!) Troll

told her everything now, how he had believed all humans were the same destroyers of nature, killers of magic and the old ways, enemies to woodland life. Child must be a trick! It didn't matter what size humans were. They were all the same.

Serenity listened, one long slender hand gently stroking a rabbit which lay asleep in her cloak. A dove sat on one of her shoulders, and a small dormouse crept into a fold in the hem of her skirt, which was woven of mosses and lichen. When Troll had finished she sighed, and all the leaves in her cloak seemed to sigh with her in red and amber waves. 'You cannot deny Child, dear Troll of Tree Hill. You cannot deny *Them* – big, or small. They are to be pitied as much as feared, and they are to be helped if all that you hold dear is to survive.'

Troll began to protest, but she raised her hand for silence. 'Humans have made mistakes,' she said. 'Unlike the beings in our nature world, they will fight each other in groups, they can create new materials of great strength for good or bad uses, and they no longer live according to the seasons or the changes of the moon. But they are creatures of this Earth, and some of them still like and need the beings of nature. Have you cast out Grey Wagtail and Hedgehog?'

Troll blushed and hung his head, and Serenity continued: 'They will be received by the kind ones, and others will follow them. You cannot divide up worlds completely. You should visit Child's world and see for yourself.' Serenity reached to the ground for something, and then, in her outstretched hand Troll could see a pine cone and a beech nut. 'Do you know what will happen to each of these by Spring?' She asked. Troll shook his head dumbly. 'They will open out gently – each of them – giving out something and changing their shape gradually.' Serenity leaned over and looked closely at Troll. 'Time to open out, Troll.' She spoke gently. Then she rose. 'Now I will prepare you a bed of soft leaves and you must sleep. You have journeyed far.' She gave him a drink made from ripe autumn fruits, and he gratefully curled up in slumber. He dreamed that Serenity covered him with soft downy blankets which became huge wings. He flew up beyond the clouds to the land of his ancestors where he was welcomed into an enormous circle of songs and warming fires. Troll Woman was there, with a basket of spring flowers. In the dream he felt strong and well, and full of happiness. The older bearded ones praised him and put their arms around him. Even the tip of his nose was warm.

How long he slept, he did not know. He awoke to a sky of night cloud, and the dark freshness of the forest. The enormous beech towered above him protectively. And next to his leafy pillow lay a pine cone, and a beech nut.

IV. Down Yonder

When all on Tree Hill learned that Troll would travel to Down Yonder a great chain of co-operation went swinging into action. Puck would seek out Robin who would find Grey Wagtail, who would know where to find Child. Grey Wagtail would tell Hedgehog to tell Fox that he was needed as a means of transport, for Troll knew he would be quite lost beyond the road. The squirrel brought him nuts and berries for his journey. Water Vole and the rabbits made a warm scarf from gathered bits of loose fur. Kingfisher even brought Troll a fish! Old Otter and Gentle Doe watched it all with a certain disbelief as their friend prepared willingly to enter forbidden territory.

It suited both Fox and Troll best to leave at dusk and travel by night. Wearing his hat and scarf, pockets bulging with provisions, Troll said his good-byes with grim determination. Then, securely astride Fox's back, and feeling positively terrified, he set out into the night. And all those left behind began nervously waiting. On that night the first light frost of the season etched its way onto leaves and bark in silver patterns.

Three days went by before Troll returned, dazed, stooped, and bedraggled. There were blue shadows under his eyes, and he blinked often – as though he was terribly tired or had simply seen too much. The new scarf had been lost, and one knee badly bruised, so that he hobbled rather than stomped. He told tales of metal boxes on spinning circles which screech and fly – no, *charge* at great speed along the ground on straight, rock-hard surfaces. 'These things make roaring noses and belch little puffs of smoke,' he said, 'and humans ride in them.' He told of tall, dead branchless trees which hold cold lights – lights that stay bright all night long and hum eerie noises across thin straight wires. He told of dark smoke and horrid thick air that was hard to breathe. And great herds of people who pushed and shoved, moving rapidly. There were incomprehensible noises coming from tiny boxes which some humans carried or placed by their ears. Whole stretches of land which had no grass, bushes, or trees. Tasteless water dripped out of funny little spouts. There were dogs which barked and cats which did not.

Some places did have grass and trees by them. Child's home did. Fox went there by twilight to look for food in the bin at the back door. Hedgehog usually found a saucer of milk there. Nuts and breadcrumbs lay on high tables for the birds. 'I saw Child,' Troll said, and what he had seen through Child's window had made him feel better; pretty pebbles in a dish, pine cones and sea shells, carved bits of wood, a spider in her web, and a candle in a candle stick. 'They light it at night,' Troll explained knowingly, 'and blow it out before sleep, just like I do.'

'Did Child see you?' they all wanted to know.

Troll crossed his arms over his chest and frowned. 'No. Child isn't alone there. It isn't just his home. There are others – two big ones, and a smaller one with long plaits and a high voice. The small one plays on the grass and climbs up into the tree there. She . . .' Troll stopped for a moment and chortled, 'she hangs from the tree branch by her legs and swings *upside down*!' Then he threw back his head and roared with laughter. The animals and birds stared as his shaking howls continued. Troll's stomach bounced up and down – he bent over and laughed and laughed. Tears streamed down his cheeks, and he held his sides, shrieking with mirth until he collapsed in a jelly-like heap, still giggling.

Tree Hill had never heard or seen anything like it before. Birds peered curiously and ruffled their feathers. The animals felt bewildered, but somehow pleased, as well. Troll sat up, wiping his eyes with his beard. 'Oh dear,' he gasped, 'Oh dear, the sight of her swinging upside down . . .' He chuckled and rocked gently. And then he lay down again and fell fast asleep on the spot. Everyone nudged, pulled

and pushed, until he was snoring soundly in his own bed, tucked in by Water Vole and safe from cold, frost, and Down Yonder. But the sound of Troll's laughter – a sound never heard before on Tree Hill – had warmed everyone. A new, satisfied calm settled over the hillside, and Grey Wagtail and Hedgehog were no longer in disgrace.

The frosts grew heavier now, curling colourful fallen leaves and turning them dry brown to better show off delicate silver-white patterns. Days grew shorter and flowed nicely, one into the other. Tree Hill was settling down for the winter.

So it was that Troll began tidying his own comfortable home, sweeping it out with a broom of dried reeds, reaching into corners with a cat-tail to clear out ancient, matted cobwebs and rotting leaves. He aired his sheepskin under the autumn sky, for it would be much needed in the months to come. Candles were stored neatly on a dry ledge, felt slippers dusted off carefully, and the clay cooking pot scrubbed clean in the stream. It was all very soothing busy-ness, indeed. Water Vole appeared with the last of the season's water-cress from further downstream, and they lunched quietly on salad.

Later that afternoon Troll began mixing mud, twigs and water so he could fill the holes and cracks in the walls of Gnarled Root House, thus keeping out unwanted cold air. Stirring steadily, first with a stick, then with his hands, he announced to no one in particular that he had learned this from beavers. 'What are beavers?' asked a listening frog.

'Beavers.' Troll stretched his mud-covered hands out towards all around him; Puck the pigeon above, the frogs, squirrel and Little Doe all drew closer to listen with interest. 'Beavers were powerful, majestic animals which lived long ago on the Stream and in the rivers too. They were shaped rather like Watervole but were much bigger and had huge, long, heavy flat tails. With their tails they would mix and pat mud into shapes like this.' He leaned over and struck his own mixture sharply, repeatedly, until some of it went firm and flat (the rest having splattered on to his nose and beard, which he didn't seem to notice).

'Beavers made dams to change water direction and cross great spans of rushing water.' Trolls voice was becoming louder as it often did when he told stories. He was addressing the trees and sky, as well, now.

Little Water Vole listened dreamily, imagining an animal shaped like herself but as big as the willow tree, with a tail so long it became a bridge over the stream. She sighed. Then, startled, she realised it wasn't Troll's voice she heard any longer, but Grey Wagtail's. The bird had flown into the circle suddenly, and was anxious.

Troll's magic beaver memory seemed to have vanished. He stood, muddy and blank looking. Then he slowly shook his head. 'No,' he said, 'it is out of the question.'

Vole waddled through the mud to Troll's side and peered up at him. 'What is out of the question? Tell us about beavers again.' An older grey squirrel pulled her gently to one side and whispered, 'Gray Wagtail brings news. Child is very ill. He says Troll must go to him to save him.'

'Save him?' Water Vole blinked her tiny eyes, not understanding. 'How can Troll save him? What about the beavers?'

'*Please*, Troll.' Grey Wagtail was pleading now, perched on Little Doe's back and jumping up and down with the urgency of it all, flapping his wings.

'NO!' thundered Troll , and mud splattered off his beard again in every direction. 'It is nothing to do with me. Get out of my sight and leave me alone!' He turned and shuffled away, shaking his head to and fro. Water Vole hurried after him, up the bank.

'Shall I bring some more mud to do the cracks ?' She asked hopefully. He did not answer, but slammed the door in her face.

The Hollow seemed to echo with his answer; 'Nothing to do with me . . . Nothing to do with me . . .' Bare branches tossed the words to mocking breezes. The very water of the Stream began to repeat the phrase, tumbling over rocks and tree roots. Underneath green water weed frogs heard it and nodded to each other. Little Doe cocked her head to one side, gently listening, and then bent to drink.

A chill fell as the afternoon light began to fade. Troll fumed away, bringing in his sheepskin and slippers. Huffing and puffing, he repeated, 'Nothing to do with me. The very thought of it – Bah!' That he should have anything to do with Child at all was utter nonsense, rubbish, balderdash. He had no connection whatsoever – hardly knew the fellow – a Human, at that! At dusk he noticed Water Vole's small form by his door and beckoned her in.

'Ridiculous,' Troll told her. 'Child falls ill and they run to me. Something wrong with his stomach, the bird says, dixapend, or dendapix, or whatever. Probably something the silly fool ate. Humans don't know the first thing about good food. Lying in bed in a pitalhosp somewhere, whatever that is.'

'Not a pitalhosp' came a faint voice from the doorway. 'A hospital.' It was Hedgehog, who entered slowly and wearily. 'Troll – he talks of you in his sleep. You are his secret, but he doesn't know if you are real or not, anymore. And he has been in terrible pain.'

'Pain?' Something glimmered in Troll's eyes. 'Pain!' He stood up, stiff as a board. 'Don't you think humans have caused enough pain to animals and all living things of Nature over the years? Don't talk to me about pain! This whole affair is of no importance to me whatsoever. Do you hear?'

Hedgehog hung his head. The whole of Tree Hill had heard. And Water Vole slipped silently away to her own safe nesting place, shivering in the darkness. Quietly, dejectedly, Hedgehog left, as well.

The full moon rose, a glowing, shining orb of blue light in a soft grey sky. Its light flooded Troll's room, bathed his bed in unwanted radiance, gave him no rest or sleep. He tossed fitfully. His thoughts haunted him, the silence of the night tormented him. He realised that he still had caked mud on his beard. His nose was cold, and so was his bald patch. Climbing out of bed, he found his woolly hat and decided to go down to the stream to wash his face and beard. Perhaps he would sleep better if he felt cleaner. The door creaked as he opened it.

What he entered was a sparkling silver wonderland in the full light of the moon. Grass and moss glistened under his feet as though covered in tiny diamonds. Troll walked as quietly as he could down to the bank, comforted by the soft gurgling of stream water. He splashed the clear, cold wetness all over his face, his beard and his nose. But he felt even more awake now. The moon seemed to remind him of something. He dried his nose on his sleeve and rubbed it thoughtfully. Then he pulled his woolly cap down over his ears and turned.

The minute the moon was at his back, he knew. It reminded him of the child-pebble . . . the marble . . . the gift he kept in his treasure corner. It was round, shining, colourful and special. Troll frowned and plodded up the path, tiny frosted twigs snapping here and there as he walked. With the moon behind him, he seemed to face a curious blue shadow as he walked – as though he was meeting a part of himself, or another version of himself against the frosty white ground. It made him feel very uncomfortable.

Troll closed his door tightly to keep the shadow outside, placed his hat in front of the little round window to do the same for the light, and climbed once more into bed. Head under his pillow, nose-warmer in place now, he muttered softly 'Nothing to do with me,' and waited for sleep. He hoped for dreams, for advice from the Old Ones. Sometimes in full daylight he would lie on his back looking upward at white billowing clouds and think he saw their shapes – the ancestors, the wise ones. Let them come now, in a dream, to tell him that everything was all right. Before he fell asleep, a single tear worked its way down Troll's nose and nose-warmer to the whiteness of his beard.

There were no dreams. He awoke feeling empty, not right. He remembered the odd blue shadow, the silence of the night. In the corner of his room, in his favourite old bird-nest basket, was the marble, a pine cone, and a beech nut. He would rest today. The moon would still be bright enough tonight to travel by. He would need to go by himself this time.

No one saw Troll leave at nightfall. Grey Wagtail had long since flown away back Down Yonder, and Hedgehog was curled into a ball, deeply asleep after her own long journey back. Troll placed the special marble in front of Water Vole's doorway so that she would understand. An owl hooted above, wishing him a safe journey, and he felt his feet growing lighter. He must do everything by day break. He must summon some Old Magic.

V. The Return

On his previous journey Troll had crossed the Road astride Fox's back, trusting Fox to move at the right time. Stealthily, swiftly, they had made their way to the safety of a hedge on the other side of the road.

To Troll now, standing alone on the ridge above this same road, it seemed an immense stretch of impassable hard dark surface. Whiffs of grey cloud, like gently billowing smoke, covered the moon and let only a tiny bit of light through. Feeling rather small in the darkness, Troll suddenly wished that he had brought his wooden sword, or perhaps a picnic. Either would have helped him feel braver. Then came a distant rumble followed by a rushing screech and roar of bright lights as a vehicle raced past. He held his ears and felt the ground shudder under his feet. The car was gone as quickly as it had come. With a cautious glance in each direction, Troll ventured forth.

He stood at the rim of it – this vast, black covering on the ground. It was quite still. He put one foot on it and winced at the cold, dark hardness of it all. Then he took several steps, holding his head high.

'BEEP – BEEP!' A thundering giant of glaring lights and roaring noise roared past him, the ensuing wind blowing off his woolly hat and sending him into a terrific spin. Troll fell into a ditch, dizzily clutching his head and feeling his heart beat so fast that it drummed painfully against his chest. He gulped. There was another zooming noise and flash of light. Then another. The road was much used tonight, and he could not cross it – he dare not. These passing thunder giants would gobble him up – they knew no mercy, never slowed down, always raced heavily past.

Nose aching, chest hurting, Troll gazed fearfully up at the sky. A single, solitary gleaming star had appeared. It sparkled for him. Clouds floated past it but did not cover it. It sparkled for him. That was it! The old magic for safe sea voyages – focus on the first star and command its light for safe crossing. He jumped to his feet hopefully, pulled his hat on again, and climbed out of the ditch.

With the wind blowing his beard and dappled moonlight all around him, Troll danced and sang, jumped, twirled and gathered his courage. Shortly after this he was well on the other side of the road. Whether by luck or magic, he was safely over. Glancing over his shoulder, he winked his thanks to the still sparkling star. Now there were a multitude of ways to manoeuvre – over a fence here, around a dark corner there, up and down kerbstones and steps. There were narrow streets through which somewhat slower light and noise rumbled now and then. Tall, shadowy structures with squares of light here and there loomed on either side of him. A dog barked and he froze, waiting for it. It didn't come.

Smells – the heavy, airless smell of roads, scents of rotting rubbish in bags and bins, peculiar odours which made his nose crinkle. When he heard footsteps Troll darted into a dark corner, peeking out only when the tall, talking humans had walked well past. Someone whirled by on a bicycle. He had learned the word 'bicycle' at Child's house. Child had one.

But where was Child's house?

Troll felt it was a long way off yet. He scampered up steps over a high footbridge gazing only briefly at the shadowy train tracks below, and then made his way down the other side, It was almost all hard, dull pavement now, with cracks and bits of paper or old tins to step over. There were tall brick walls on either side of him, and slowly he began to feel quite lost. The glowing green eyes of a cat confronted him momentarily, but the animal turned noiselessly and ran away. He realised that there were pigeons roosting on rafters in a tumble-down building not far away. Perhaps they would know which way he should go. Clouds completely covered the moon as he stepped over rubbish and puddles, approaching the leaning wooden walls in total darkness. There was broken glass on the ground, and a stench such

as he had never known. Grey bags and bundles lay up against the wall. Perhaps he could stand on one to approach the pigeons. Perhaps these were bales of hay in an untidy, smelly barn.

But to Troll's horror one of the bags moved and mumbled, and a human arm reached out, holding a bottle. Another bag sat up in a huddled heap – so close that Troll could see his face and smell foul breath. The face was bearded and covered in scraggly locks of hair. Furthermore, the face was only half-awake. 'Hey Half-Pint' said its gravelly voice. In terror, Troll turned to run – 'Hey Shorty!' came the voice again, 'Where'ya going on a cold night with no coat. Have a coat, Stranger.' He tossed a crumpled garment towards Troll which landed at his feet. Then he took a long drink from his bottle, rolled over and mumbled something unclear. Snores followed. The human was asleep.

Troll swayed slightly feeling almost sick with relief. Then he examined the coat. Would it be a useful disguise? Could he pass as a small human by night?

With feathers fluttering, a grey pigeon settled on the pavement beside him. 'You're not from these parts.' She chirped.

'I am Troll of Tree Hill.' He rose to his full height and stood straight. But pigeon was not impressed, or even interested. She picked a crumb from a crumpled paper plate in the gutter and flew upward again.

'Please,' Troll called after her, 'please, which way is it to Child's house?' The pigeon did not answer, but two bundled men stirred and muttered at the sound of his voice. Troll picked up the coat and backed carefully away into the street and its shadows. He tried on the coat. It had a musty smell and fell down well past his feet. But he felt curiously protected in it. Plodding steadily along, Troll advanced into town.

Lighting was more regular in the lanes he entered now. He thought he recognised a bin where Fox had stopped to forage. It stood next to a bench by a hedge. Troll brightened – yes, Child's home was

on a small road near the park. The park was a square of grassland with a few spindly trees and some strange objects for small humans to play on. But the sound of heavy footsteps startled Troll out of his happy recognition. He waddled into the hedge and hid there, wrapped in the great, warm coat.

A tall human dressed in dark clothes with bright metal buttons and badge strolled past, a long stick in one hand, a hat on his head. He stepped firmly, whistling, looking this way and that, and then came to a stop in the light of the street lamp by the bin. Troll feared that the human would sit on the bench next, thus trapping him behind. But then he heard shorter, quicker steps, and a new figure bustled into view.

'Evening Mrs Perkins.' The first human tipped his hat. 'You're out late this evening.'

The shorter figure was fairly round and wore a head scarf. 'Yes Officer. It's my cleaning night at the hospital and I've left me bag behind. I'm going back for it. It's got the shopping in it for tomorrow, you know.'

The tall one nodded, and they stood chatting for a while.

Huddled in the protection of the leafy hedge, Troll frowned. Hospital. Was that what Hedgehog had said? Could it be that Child was not at his house, or could hospital be the same thing? He was confused now, and slightly cramped as well! Finally the two figures parted, each going a different way down the pavement. Awkwardly, Troll pulled himself out of his hiding spot, disentangling his beard from spiky branches and shaking his head free of leaves. The moon was high and clear now; he noted this gratefully, rubbing his nose in thought. He would follow Mrs Perkins. He scampered after her, coat flying behind him, fists clenched anxiously. She turned a corner and so did he, narrowly missing another lamp post. They were everywhere. You would hardly know it was night-time. He fairly flew now, determined not to lose Mrs Perkins from view. But the long hem of the swirling coat caught his foot. Down he tumbled and rolled. 'Oh fuss and bother' he shouted, quite forgetting where he was. 'Oh bother and fuss!' Bruised and fuming, he rose to his feet, picked up the heavy lengths of brown coat and staggered on.

Then Troll stopped in his tracks, utterly astounded. An enormous long vehicle with lighted windows and many wheels had stopped for the human he was chasing. A door slid open, she disappeared through it, and with a huge gasping noise and the familiar, awful road smell, it sped off – taking her with it! Stunned, he sat down on the cold pavement. It was as though she had been eaten up before his very eyes. Now what? Would such a thing come and eat him next?

Through his daze Troll became vaguely aware of soft chuckling. He peered into the darkness to see Robin perched on a fence nearby. Robin flew over to him. 'What a comical sight you make tonight, Troll.' The little bird hugged his red breast with short wings, doubled up in chirpy laughter. When he had caught his breath again he explained, 'It's only a bus – a city bus and its load of people. They stop there frequently.'

Troll shook his head and stroked his beard. 'I'll be worn out by morning. I must find Child tonight. I must find the hospital!'

Robin perched on his shoulder. 'I can take you to Child's house if that helps.'

With relief Troll followed him, winding his way through the park. They reached the darkened cottage, and Troll found the trellis he had used before. He climbed it clumsily, and peered into the window of the room that was Child's. It was empty. A pair of shoes lay on the floor, bed-clothes had been left in a muddle, and one forlorn sock lay over the back of a wooden chair. Little frost flowers were etched into the window pane around the clear circle Troll had rubbed for peeking through.

Wearily, he climbed back down and slumped on to the dark cold ground. Robin spoke encouragingly – 'You could follow the bus to the hospital.'

Troll moaned. 'It goes too fast. I'd never keep up with it. I've come all this way for nothing.'

'I know!' Robin flew up and down in excitement. 'Borrow Child's bicycle. Follow the bus on a bicycle and you'll go just as fast. Try it!'

'But –'

'Use your magic, Troll!' Robin pulled him gently by the beard to a shed behind the house. There, basking in moonlight, was the old red bicycle.

Exactly half an hour later (by human measure) Troll careened down the street, wobbling to and fro, unsteadily but almost fearlessly. His beard flew in the wind, the end of his nose was quite warm in all

the excitement (in spite of crisp, cold night air) and Robin clung to his woolly hat. The small bird chirped directions merrily, and soon they were trailing the enormous bulky bus from corner to corner, each time it stopped or started the huge yawning, gasping noise came before it trundled on again. People got on and off, not noticing the curious couple in the darkness well behind.

Troll didn't know how far they had come – he had no sense of direction or distance in this place of brick and cement and straight lines. There were no familiar shapes, patterns, or sounds. But finally the bus stopped yet another time and a voice from inside it boomed 'City Hospital'.

'Robin,' whispered Troll rather urgently, 'how do I stop the bicycle?'

He needn't have asked. City Hospital was atop a hill and the bicycle slowed down immediately on the sudden upward slope, allowing Troll and friend to clamber off it. But Hospital itself loomed from the hill in a blaze of light, an enormous tall straight-up-and-down building with so many lines of tiny windows that Troll felt quite dizzy just looking. What appeared to be an entire field of cars was next to it, and he could hear voices and footsteps come from this direction. Apparently hospitals didn't sleep at night.

Robin coughed nervously. 'Time I went back to the house garden. Good luck now.' And he flew off.

Troll blinked in disbelief at the towering structure ahead. He felt tiny, cold and lost. The night seemed unfriendly and full of sinister shadows. Then to his relief he spied another form next to the hospital. It was a tall, stately and ancient Oak tree. It seemed to beckon – even sing to him with its branches. He set the bicycle down on the now frozen ground and stumbled towards the tree.

Just to feel the bark was reassuring. To sit in the rough, twisting roots was security, itself. Troll shuddered, wrapping his arms and coat around himself, cap pulled down to cover his eyes and almost his nose. He tried to imagine Tree Hill at night, the smells of damp, rich earth, the sounds of rushing water and breezes in treetops. He rocked himself gently, thinking of his own cosy bed, the soft glow

from his candle in the brass candle stick. Then he felt familiar bumpy acorn shapes beneath him and remembered suddenly that it was ages since he had eaten anything.

The acorns were good. Munching them helped him face the shock of lights from the hospital, but now he wondered how – in all that – he would ever find Child. He broke the thin ice covering a pool of rain water caught in a crevice in the tree. Refreshed by this cold drink, Troll peered earnestly at the sky.

So many unreal lights gave off a reflection of sorts into the darkness so that an orange haze clouded the night. But above that, if he looked far enough and long enough, he could see friendly wisps of cloud. And there, far above him, twinkled the lone star. Troll smiled in delight. The star sparkled and shone. One beam of silver seemed to bounce continuously off a particular window high up in the hospital. Troll's eyes followed the beam from star to window, and he nodded. The black night sky was just beginning to turn to dark blue, with a faint streak of red appearing behind the distant rooftop horizon. It had been a long, eventful night, and it was not yet over. Troll summoned all the Old Magic he could, thanked the mighty Oak for his rest stop, and crossed the grass to the hospital wall. He positioned himself under the starlight and began climbing. Using feet, hands and nose, he worked himself up brickwork, past window ledges and a series of drain pipes, steadily, painstakingly. His heart thumped madly as he went higher and higher, the ground so far below. Each movement took enormous effort. He was almost at his target window when he nearly slipped on an icy patch. He caught his balance, breathed deeply, and pulled himself up again. Toes secure between bricks, he grasped the window ledge and peered unsteadily over it.

There, in a softly lit but still dazzling white room, in a white bed under white covers, lay Child. He seemed to be asleep, but in pain, or certainly frowning. His dark hair looked damp on the white pillow. Troll stood precariously on the ledge and tried to lift open the window. It opened just a crack, enough for him to tap and whisper 'Child, Child! It's me – Troll of Tree Hill. We met in the Wood. Child?'

The weak form in the bed tossed his head back and forth, eyes closed. Troll tugged again at the window until it jerked open slightly, nearly losing his balance in the process. He squeezed himself through the wide crack.

The room had curious smells and the whiteness of it was quite overwhelming. But Troll ignored this, and leaned over to whisper in Child's ear. His beard must have tickled, for Child's eyes flew open. An enormous smile came slowly over his face. 'Dear Troll' he whispered, 'you are real'.

Troll cleared his throat gruffly. 'I am Troll of Tree Hill' he said, 'and you must get well. The animals are very worried about you . . . ' He opened the boy's limp hand, placed three acorns in the palm, and then closed it again. The unmistakable sound of footsteps came from somewhere outside Child's door. Troll ducked quickly under the bed, but the footsteps passed by, fading away into stillness. Somewhat awkwardly, he re-emerged.

Child was pale, but his smile was radiant. 'Your nose isn't blue anymore,' he said.

Troll reached out to feel the end of his nose. 'No, er . . . climbing walls is very good for warming noses.'

The boy giggled, a faint blush creeping into his thin cheeks now. Troll beamed, ever so pleased with himself. Then, glancing at the window he saw that the sky was becoming lighter. He shook Child's hand warmly and turned to crawl out again. Later Nurse would be upset to find the window open, but delighted that her patient's fever had broken. As for Child he never doubted his healing dream because of the three acorns hidden safely under the mattress.

Troll stumbled to the ground just at sunrise and headed weakly for the Oak tree. Pale morning colours bathed him as he lay down to rest in the safety of tree roots. He was utterly exhausted now . . . and relieved in a light, tingly – almost floating way. It was as though years and years of heaviness and loneliness had been lifted from him. Since the passing of the other Trolls he had been so very alone.

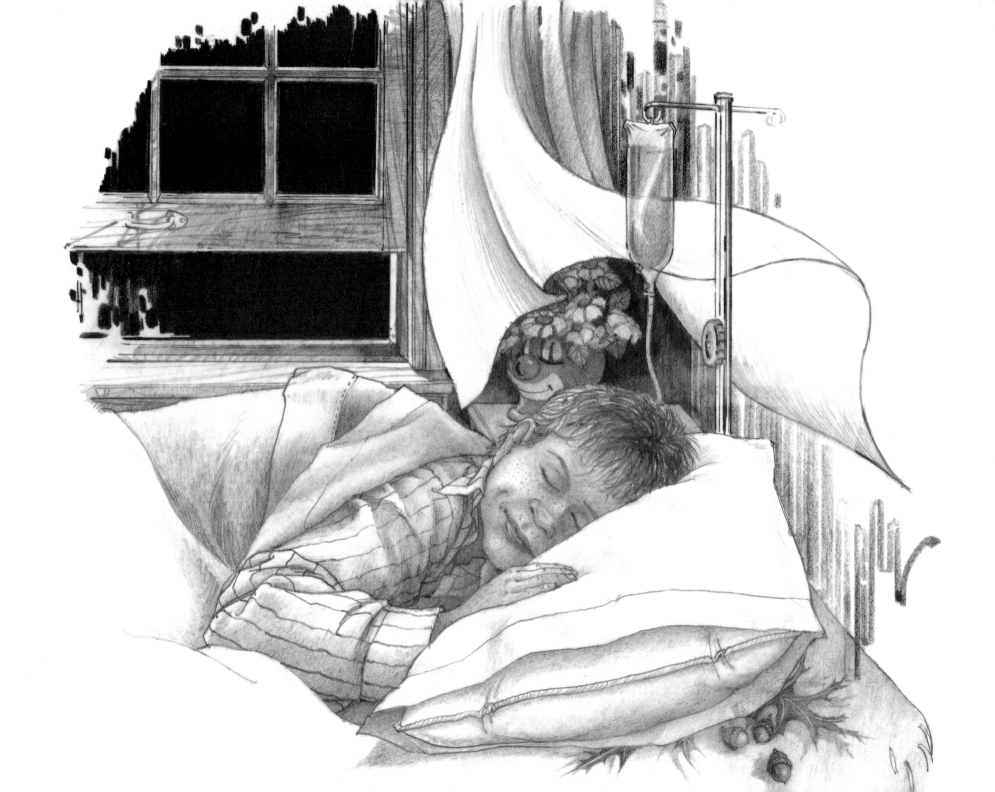

He loved the creatures of Tree Hill dearly but felt such a responsibility to look after them. Had he built walls around himself with his old fears and hatred? Child had reached out to him, breaking down those walls. He had been able to reach back to Child.

In either sleep or a trance he imagined himself being lifted up on red and orange dawn carpets – carried upward to the cheers and warmth and music of the Wise Ones. In coral light they cheered him, lifted him up on a sea of happy troll faces, placed him in a warm circle of blazing fires. Troll Woman was there with spring flowers. 'You've done well, Troll of Tree Hill,' they all chorused. And billowing clouds of rainbow colours and music enveloped him, welcomed him, claimed him.

Little Doe said to Hedgehog and Watervole and Puck the Pigeon, 'He's not coming back, is he? No, but he is here all the same, isn't he.' And they all nodded, wide-eyed at both thoughts, watching the morning sky with mixed feelings of loss and contentment. Water Vole showed the Child-pebble before hiding it safely in the Willow bank. Later that day the first snowflakes of the season fell, swirling steadily down in lazy circles, and by dusk the wood lay covered in a soft white blanket. They all felt the graceful gliding of Serenity's figure that night, dusting Troll's door with a shower of tiny stars, raising her strong hands first to the treetops and then to the skies and singing in a voice sweeter than wild honey. She sang of realms and futures the animals could only blink and hear about, then gently knelt to touch each creature in smiling blessing before she left. There was no frost on the door of Gnarled Root House, and a single rose bloomed above it. Tree Hill entered its glistening white winter slumber, gratefully, silently dreaming of Spring.

hild grew up. He studied trees and plants and became someone people looked up to. People came to him with questions about growing things. He worked with other people to stop a new road going through Tree Hill and found ways to protect it and Upper Wood, as well. Otters appeared in greater numbers along the stream, as did deer – for the first time in many years. Even the heron came back to fish again in its waters. There was another route around the hill which would leave Nature unharmed, but still allow people rapid travel to other cities if that was what they wanted.

Sometimes he led walks up the hill towards the Hollow, telling groups about the plants and animals of the Wood. In town he kept a large garden, and later a large family as well. He told his children stories at night about elves, fairies and trolls – about magic and the unseen life in nature's hiding places. It was a family rich in stories and laughter. The stories and laughter seemed to help the children grow as much as good food or enough sleep.

One Spring day his eldest daughter walked with him to the Stream, lined as it was on either side with waves of bluebells and soft new green. There, at the foot of a graceful willow tree, she spied something light in the damp and mossy earth. It was a blue and white marble. Carefully she wiped it on her coat sleeve until it shone in the sunlight. 'I wonder how long that has been there,' she exclaimed.

'About thirty years, I should think,' answered her father. Then he led her down the stream. By the side of the swirling water they discovered two comfortable stone shapes, formed almost like short squat figures. Yellow flags grew by the stones, and behind them another sea of bluebells. There were clumps of primroses and tiny violets. There in the coolness of a late April day, to the music of bird song and breezes, he told her a new story.

And now you know it, as well.